Seahorses Are Sold Out

This edition first published in 2021 by Gecko Press
PO Box 9335, Wellington 6141, New Zealand
info@geckopress.com

English-language edition © Gecko Press Ltd 2021
Translation © Shelley Tanaka 2021
Title of the original German edition: *Seepferdchen sind ausverkauft*
Illustrations: Katja Gehrmann
Text: Constanze Spengler
© 2020 Moritz Verlag, Frankfurt am Main
English-language edition arranged through mundt agency, Düsseldorf

Distributed in the United States and Canada by Lerner Publishing Group, lernerbooks.com
Distributed in the United Kingdom by Bounce Sales and Marketing, bouncemarketing.co.uk
Distributed in Australia and New Zealand by Walker Books Australia, walkerbooks.com.au

The translation of this work was supported by a grant from the Goethe-Institut.

Edited by Penelope Todd
Cover design by Vida Kelly
Typesetting by Esther Chua
Printed in China by Everbest Printing Co. Ltd, an accredited ISO 14001 & FSC-certified printer

ISBN hardback: 978-1-776573-85-1
ISBN paperback: 978-1-776573-86-8
Ebook available

For more curiously good books, visit geckopress.com

Katja Gehrmann
and Constanze Spengler

SEAHORSES ARE
SOLD OUT

Translated by Shelley Tanaka

GECKO PRESS

"Are we going to the lake today?" I ask.

"No," says Dad. "Not today."

"But you promised!"

"I know, Mika. But I have to finish this first." He rummages on his desk.

"How long will it take?"

"I don't know. But if you let me work in peace, it will be a lot quicker."

I let him work in peace and only ask now and then,
"How much longer?"
"Can't you go and play?" he says.
"No. It's boring by myself."
"Call next door. I'm sure Karli will play with you."
"Karli's gone to stay with his grandma," I say.
"She has a dog."

I've wanted a dog or a cat or even a mouse
for absolute ages, but Dad says no.
I ask again anyway. "Can I have a pet?"

Dad looks as if he's thinking about it.
"Can I?!"
"If you did have a pet…would you play with it very quietly
and not bother me until I finish my work?"
"Yes!" I shout.

Dad gives me his wallet and tells me to watch out for traffic.

Pet Kingdom is just around the corner.
I pick out a mouse, but the pet store man
wants to check with my father.

Dad doesn't like being disturbed.
"*Of course* Mika can have a mouse!" I hear
him shout over the phone. "Just sell the kid
whatever, and now please let me get on
with my work!"

I set up the cage in the living room and make
it comfy for the mouse.
I play with him all afternoon. He loves tunnels
and hiding places, so I build lots of them.

The next morning, I can't find the mouse.
My hiding places were too good.
I ask Dad for help.
"Go and ask at the pet store," he says.
"They'll know what to do."

There are new puppies in the store. The man says dogs have such sensitive noses they can sniff out anything.

I buy a puppy.

The puppy finds the mouse before I can
even take off my shoes.

The three of us play tag in the living room
until Dad calls me for dinner.
"Did you find the mouse?" he asks.
"Yes," I say. "No problem."
"Good," he says. "Make sure he
doesn't escape again."

Before I go to bed, I take the puppy to the bathroom and explain how to use the toilet. I tell her to take good care of the mouse while I'm asleep.

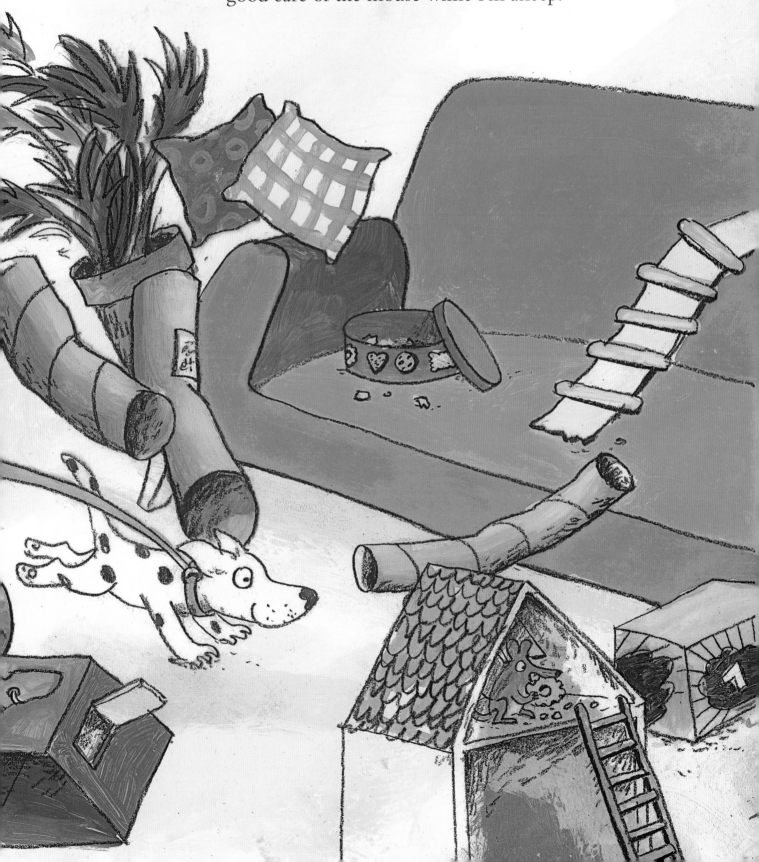

Next morning, the mouse is still in the cage, twitching his nose.
"Good job," I tell the puppy.

"Listen," says Dad at breakfast, "I had to clean up the bathroom this
morning. Someone made a puddle beside the toilet."
I guess the puppy didn't understand my instructions. She is practically
still a baby.
"It can happen when you're little," I tell Dad.
"Okay," he sighs. "It's not that bad."

He disappears into his office.

Luckily, I know how to solve the toilet problem...
I saw a seal in the pet shop. She's already quite big. She can live in
the bathroom and make sure everyone uses the toilet properly.

In the afternoon we splash around in the bathtub. The mouse doesn't want to. He can't swim. He needs someone to teach him.

I run back to the pet store. The seahorses are sold out, but there is a little penguin. She teaches the mouse to swim. The rest of us work on our diving.

"What are you up to in there?" Dad calls from his office.
"My mouse is learning to swim!"
"Well don't go too wild. And wipe the floor when you're done."

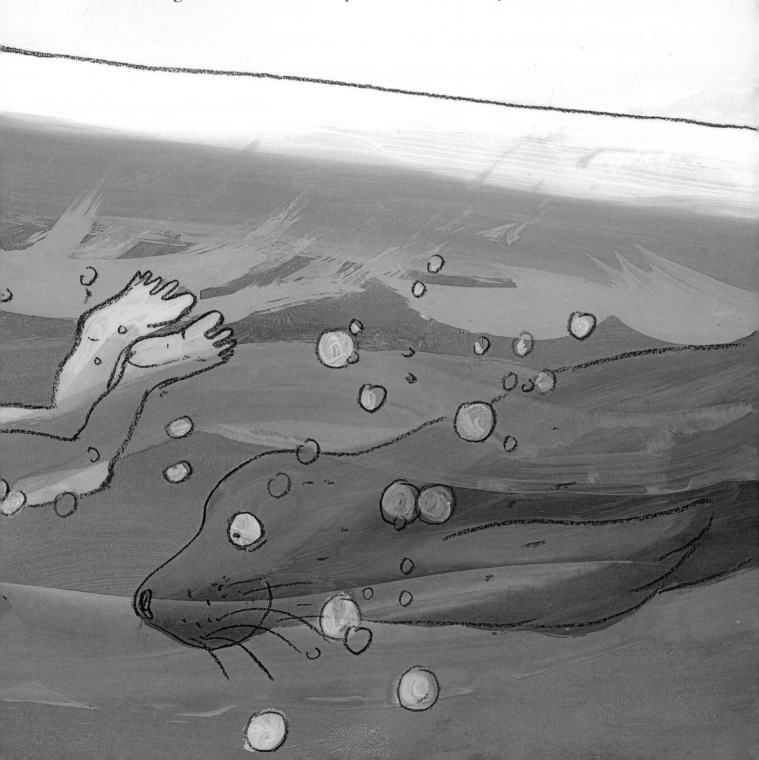

The penguin only wants to watch TV. We hang out
on the sofa and watch animal shows all day long.

At some point Dad calls from his office that I should turn it off.
"Too much TV isn't good for you," I tell the penguin.

The penguin sulks in the sink. The seal and I try to cheer her up,
but she turns on the water so she can't hear us.
"I think she misses the other birds," I say. "That's why she wants to
watch animal shows."

The mouse, the puppy and I go to the pet store for another bird.
The seal stays home to make sure the penguin doesn't turn on the TV.

The pet store man shows us a beautiful parrot. "He belonged
to a sea captain, so he knows the sea and speaks very well."
"The penguin will like that," I say.

Next day we play sailors in the living room.

Our ship is the sofa and the parrot gives the orders:

"All hands on deck!" he calls. "Heave ho, me hearties!"

We're in a tornado when Dad comes from the kitchen with his mug of tea.

"Can you keep it down in here?" he says.

"Batten the hatch, you scurvy seadog!" the parrot shrieks.

"Now, listen here, I'm trying to work." Dad gives me a stern look,
even though I haven't said a thing.
I give him a stern look back. "When will you be finished?"
"Soon," says Dad. Then his phone rings, and we don't see him
for the rest of the day.

Pet
Kingdom

I go and tell the pet store that Dad doesn't like the way the parrot talks to him.

"No problem," says the man. "I have a young elephant who's exceptionally musical. When the parrot gets too cheeky, she'll drown him out."

I buy the elephant. And because I'm a regular customer, I'm given a sack of elephant food for free.

On Sunday morning, the animals and I have been up for ages
by the time Dad comes in for breakfast.

"Good morning," I say.

"Morning, Mika." He smiles. "I worked through the night,
and I'm finished at last. Today we can finally go to the lake."

"That's great!" I say. "But…"

"…can my animals come too?"

Dad and I agree that the only thing missing is a seahorse.